# RED EAGLE ANTHOLOGY

ERIC KERCHER

PAPER AND SWORD, LLC

# Contents

# From the Author

There are days when we all need an escape from a terrible job, a terrible day, or a terrible life.

Join my newsletter and get an escape from the real world, stories, and lore designed to entertain and delight.

You'll also get *Stories from the Deep*, an exclusive, unpublished anthology chock full of extra epilogues, short stories, and lore from the Patmos Sea Fantasy Adventure Series.

Join now at erickercher.com.

Enjoy the book.

-Eric Kercher

# Introduction

We live in an age of conflict, but there have been ages of conflict before and there will be ages of conflict afterward.

These stories explore that conflict, and the men who participate in them. After they were written I noted a common theme that ran through them.

All of them, from the lowest to the highest, abhor the violence they participate in. Some have a stronger reaction, others less so, but they all have a resistance to the life they lead.

And yet, puzzlingly, they still enact violence. They still fight, and kill, and die. Why is that?

There is a calling to violence on occasion. When the weak are being attacked, only the strong can protect them. Aggressors choose to attack for various reasons, and sometimes the only thing that will stop them is violence.

As you read the stories of these men, take them for who they are. They are good and evil, peaceful and warmongering. Like the rest of us, they are flawed and many seem to be looking for a different answer the question they all ask themselves.

And for those who search for it, my hope and prayer is that they find peace.

Eric Kercher

# 1

## INFANTRYMAN

The wind kicked up the frost, flinging it into his eyes. Steve stamped his feet, trying to get the feeling back in them, ignoring the bite of the morning and the smell of his companions.

They had been in the field far too long, and he worried today might be the last.

Still, there was a beauty to it. The rising sun sending sparkles of beauty shining into the air, the standards that waved and were pulled, clicking together, by the wind.

And the taste of anticipation in the air, mixed with the deep taste of dusty frost kicked up.

"You hear that?" someone said farther down the line.

"Silence in the ranks," the sergeant bellowed. But he heard it.

A distant tramp, footsteps led on with a willing leader. They grew louder, and the dust cloud on the horizon joined it. Steve tightened his grip on his spear, clutching at the cool wood.

Soon the enemy army appeared, standards fluttering, bearing the red eagle. There were more of them than he'd expected.

"Each man will do his duty," the captain was saying, walking up and down the line of them. "We shall wrench the head from that eagle and tear it apart limb from limb. Let no one say the lion can't fight in his own land, and let everyone bear the fighting of three men. For Unarcia!"

"Unarcia!" they shouted, a cheer rising in the air. The archers strung their bows behind the infantry, unwrapping them from the oilcloths that protected them. Gentle twangs sounded as they tested them, leading to more anticipation.

The enemy army formed up into a rank, stretching farther than the lion's.

"We might have trouble," Bill whispered to Steve.

"Not if I have anything to say about it. I'll have my pay and I can't do that if I'm dead." Steve grinned at him and lowered his visor.

The two armies faced each other, riders issued from both sides. They met in the valley, talking about something.

The chill of the morning was receding, the warmth of the sun warming his face. Steve tried to listen, but the wind scattered the voices.

Being on the front lines had its advantages, and seeing that the talk wasn't going well was one of them.

The two sides bickered, then parted, each riding to his own line.

"Battle is on then," Steve said. The orders rippled down, and the horns blew. The enemy drums sounded their signal, and the enemy advanced.

"Here we go," Bill said as they were ordered forward, letting the enemy reach the valley first.

Arrows flew over their head, the first volley striking down foot soldiers and infantry, but they simply reformed ranks and left the injured and dead behind.

One man had his shield up and blocked an arrow, which Steve found lucky. A few seconds later, he wasn't so lucky when another arrow caught him in the eye.

That familiar tightness formed up in Steve's stomach, and his legs told him to turn tail and run, but he stayed in place. Even if he did run, there was nowhere to go.

So, he swallowed the bile rising in his throat and trembled at the order. "Advance," the captain yelled.

He put one foot in front of the other, pushed forward by the throng of bodies behind and the threat of punishment above him.

He yelled, a low rumble, that was repeated up and down the line. The eyes of the enemy were visible now, hard veteran and terrified rookie that watched them come.

The yards closed, and the distance collapsed. A shining figure in glittering mail on a horse rode behind the others, accompanied by a retinue that bore the standard.

But then it was all gone, as Steve could only see the enemy in front of him. The line broke into a run, carried downhill by momentum, and the order given for spear.

He lowered his and charged, gripping on and feeling the tremors through his cold and frozen feet.

A few feet left. Then, none.

His spear felt resistance, then continued as he crashed into a sword-wielding eagle. Then confusion reigned as he pulled free his own sword, his spear stuck and lost in whoever had been on the receiving side of it.

Lungs on fire and heart pounding, Steve narrowly avoided a sword aimed at his head. Ducking, he followed up with his own slash, catching the man in the throat and sending a splash of blood through a guttural cry.

He didn't stop. Metal ground upon metal around him, screams and horrible cries of pain lancing through it all. Steve pressed forward, driven by those at his back, and waded into the others.

Hacking with his sword, he advanced a few steps forward. The enemy was wary of his strength and height, of which he used generously.

A challenger stepped forward, attacking on his backswing. Steve brought up his shield and deflected it, the vibration traveling up his arm as it collided. In the moment he couldn't feel it, and brought his sword around to stab into the surprised man's neck.

Beside him Bill kept up, exchanging blows with another swordsman.

Steve didn't feel anything then, let his hearing slip away. There was nothing but pain and anger coursing through him in a wave.

No smell of blood and death. No taste of iron. No feeling of sword upon flesh and shoulder upon shoulder.

He kept fighting, desperate just to stay alive and protect his companions to either side.

A flash, and the enemy parted to the right of them. A horse charged in, leading a retinue with it, but then the lines closed up again and Steve lost sight of it.

Over and over he fought, and his arms felt like jelly in the churned up mud, thick with brown blood.

Then a horn sounded. It was unusual, from the other side. They were retreating, falling back in a wave.

Steve felt pain now, the cuts and wounds that came with it as it caught up to him in a moment of rest. But then he was swept up, caught in the wave of pursuit as they wounded and killed those who straggled or turned to fight them.

A cheer rose up from the army, from hoarse throats and wounded lips. The enemy was retreating. They were saved.

There were more than a few that were still left alive, and then the enemy was gone, fallen back out of the range of arrows and the halt sounded.

Steve stopped then, sinking to his knees to catch his breath and still his beating heart. The ground was cold and ice against his knees, and he had a cut on the left side of his arm that trailed blood.

Vultures descended on the battlefield, crying out their mirth as they fed upon the dead. Now the smells caught up to him and he gagged, emptying his little water back onto the ground.

"We survived, Bill," Steve said, clapping him on the shoulder. His left eye was closed, the lids opened with a hideous slash.

"Aye, that we did," Bill said, rising back up on wobbly feet. Strength returned to him as they picked what they could from the dead.

Purses, trinkets, treasures. They slipped them into folds in their clothing before the sergeant got to them with his club like he was doing with the others.

"Back, you thieves. You'll get your pay, don't you worry." A stream of curses uttered from the man's lips as he beat a too-bold thief, the crack of breaking bones as he clubbed his hand. The man cried out, dropped his loot, and limped off before he could be caught and put on trial.

"Back to camp, both of you," the sergeant growled, then hurried off to have at another.

There was no mirth, no pleasure in this victory. A few of the men didn't make it, empty holes in the formation that would be filled or collapsed however the King saw fit.

Once they had picked their way through the slippery and steaming field, the hill had solidified with frost. The sun hung high in the sky, but it had felt like only a few minutes.

"Can't get over this," Steve muttered.

"Aye. So much death," Bill said. "But we'll be compensated, make no mistake."

"What good are a few gold coins when your life is at stake?"

"Don't talk like that. We're doing a good thing here." Steve swept his hands along the battlefield. "Clearing out invaders and keeping our lands safe."

"Whose lands do we protect? I have no lands, no country." Steve felt the wind flutter his hair, tickling his scalp.

"Your native homeland, that's what you protect."

Steve didn't reply, but stewed in misery and anger. He wanted to go back to the farm, work the soil and till the land.

And he wanted it to be his. When would that be possible? Would it ever be possible?

The ground crunched underfoot, his arm starting to throb. There was going to be a celebration tonight, he would think about that and that alone.

The ale would flow, the best wines brought out, and for a few moments, the world would slip away and be easy.

The camp was ordered chaos when they came in, and they split to go back to their own tents.

Steve slipped into his, stripping his bloody mail and shirt off and dropping it. He would get the camp women to wash it later, if he had enough coin.

For now, he had his wounds to tend to. Steve tore off strips of bandaging and wrapped it around the inflamed flesh, tightening it with a twist that poured fresh blood from it.

The pain over, he put on new clothes and joined the others at the fire. They had already opened the ale, and Steve took his mug.

"Come along Steve, drink deep tonight," Bill said. The warm ale washed down his throat, clearing it of the muck and blood of the battle. It was good, and hit his stomach with a happy bubble.

A few rounds later the laughter flowed. Bill started to jig, breaking forth in song about a lusty barmaid and her insatiable thirst, and had the others roaring in delight.

This was a night to forget everything he wanted, to put it off. Steve gazed into the sky, the twinkling of the stars swimming in view, and drank from the thick foam.

A rush ran through him. He had survived. He breathed deep of the smoke and smells of the camp.

He had survived.

# 2

## BLACK TROUBLE

The fire raged, bellowing smoke and heat that licked my body and sent streams of sweat flowing. Each hammer blow seemed to take more out of me, each seemed to strike as true as I thought it could.

Jacob worked the bellows, breathing hard and sending in the rich air that flamed the small fire into a raging inferno.

The metal cooled to gray. I plunged it back into the fire and stood back, catching my breath.

"Two more," I said. The metal heated, turning red and then orange, then the white hot I needed.

Out came the metal, straight onto the anvil, and I pounded it out. Sweat was on my lips, salty and sooty, and droplets of it sprayed and hissed as it hit the cooling iron.

My hammer rang out through the blacksmith, ringing in my ears, but I was absorbed in my work.

The sword was starting to take form, thinned out from the ingot that had begun its life. Now it needed straightening, and I tapped it into place.

It had cooled too much, so I put it back in. "Tend the fire after this."

"Yes, sire," Jacob said, still working the bellows. He was a good apprentice, and I was glad to have him. He still needed many more years of instruction though.

While the metal heated I glanced over at the pile of orders yet to be made. It was getting bigger, shoes for the farmers, nails for the carpenters. But I had to stop to make this.

What good were swords to the world? I considered stopping, putting it on hold, but knew I couldn't.

It was ready again, and I worked it. I drew the metal into form, taking care to flatten it and make it straight all at the same time.

It was tricky work I wasn't used to, but when the lord of the manor asks you to make a sword, you make one.

We worked into the night, but it still wasn't done.

"That's enough for now Jacob." I stretched my aching arms and back. "Damp down the fire, we'll need to get up early tomorrow to finish."

"Yes, sire." Jacob worked to clean as I finished preparing my tools for the morning. I left him sweeping the smithy and walked back in the night to my home.

The door squeaked as I opened it, and my wife stirred. "Jim, is that you?"

"Hush, it's me," I whispered. The breathing of the children was deep and steady. I stripped off my clothes, got ready, and joined my wife, grateful for the warmth after the cool of the night against my skin.

"You're late," she chided.

"I haven't finished yet."

There was a long pause. "Will you?"

"It'll be done. Sleep now." I kissed her cheek, and she caressed my face. Sleep came easy, and I dreamed.

The cock woke me in the morning, the sunlight just beginning to shine in yellows and oranges through the window.

I got up quietly, dressed, and splashed ice cold water on my face to wake myself up. I munched on a bit of stale bread from last night, better with butter, and left before anyone else was up.

Jacob was already there. "Good morning, sire."

"Good morning Jacob." The fire was starting to lick back up, eagerly eating the charcoal Jacob had fed it. Everything was tidy and in its place. "Off we go."

We picked back up where we'd left off. I knew my neighbors wouldn't like the noise, but there was nothing to be done about it.

Without a break, we worked until noon. Stephanie dropped off some lunch with the children and checked in on our progress.

"It's taking longer than I'd hoped." I glanced up the road. Empty, for now.

"Be strong," she said, squeezing my muscled arm. I nodded.

They left and after a quick meal we got back to work.

At last I was satisfied and plunged the sword into the oil to quench. It hissed and steamed, the smell of burnt oil overwhelming.

It took less time to sharpen, attach the hilt I had made earlier, and polish it. When we were done, I held it up.

It caught the rays of the fire, reflecting them like the sun. Jacob did a good job with the polishing and it was as clear as a reflective pool in the shade.

I wrapped it carefully, and turned to other work. Jacob made nails as I made the accompanying shoes.

The distant sound of galloping took me from my work. I checked the sun, only a few hours past noon.

It wasn't to be helped. Glad of the early start, I washed my hands of soot and grime in a bucket as they rode up.

"You're early," I said.

The man frowned as he dismounted. "We are on time. You'd better have it ready." There was a sneer on his face and an arrogant touch to his voice.

I nodded to Jacob, who fetched the cloth wrapped parcel. The man looked disappointed, and it made me feel better.

I don't know how long Saul had worked for the lord of the manor, but it hadn't been long. Ever since then, things had changed around here. Life was harder now, and we all knew why.

The big, burly guards that surrounded Saul may have had something to do with it. They were foreigners, mercenaries I guessed, and knew not our ways.

I handed the sword to Saul, who took it and tossed back the cloth. He examined its edge, squinting, then took it outside to hold it up to the horizon.

The examination took longer than I wanted, and I was holding my breath the whole time. My heart beat with anticipation and I willed it to slow.

"Humph." He wrapped it back up and nodded to one of his men, who took off a purse and threw it to the ground at my feet. "I'm not sure the lord will be pleased, pray that he is."

I kept my face still and silent. He wouldn't have the satisfaction he was seeking. They turned and galloped away, kicking up dust that rolled through the village and bothered my eyes.

"Sire?" Jacob's eyes were questioning.

"Back to work Jacob." I watched them go a while longer, feeling the heat of the fire at my back. Above, storm clouds gathered. "We have work to do."

# 3

# ARCHER

"I'll be taking the prize home, you wait and see." Stan rifled through his arrows, examining the fletching and brushing through the feathers.

Aidan grunted, leaning on his bow. He was in no mood to talk. A brisk wind made him shiver, and he wished for the coming of day more than ever.

"March all night, break camp before the dawn. I'm telling you, we'll see the enemy this morning." The standards of the lion fluttered in the early stirrings of the morning wind.

In the east the sun was starting to kiss the sky, the black of night brightening to gray. Aidan squeezed his hands, trying to get the circulation back into them.

The horses were too close, he could smell them. They reminded him of home, and he hated it. He would rather be back hunting rabbit on an early morning day like this.

Instead, he was here, hunting man.

Aidan let Lucas prattle on, as Kieran nudged him and pointed over to the right. "Brought up the cavalry on our flank. Doesn't look good."

"Why do you say that?"

"Mean's the big man's nervous. Wants to have them on hand when the time's needed." Kieran blew into his cupped hands, then stomped his feet against the cold. "They must be throwing everything they've got at us."

Aidan snorted. "You're a general now?"

"No, but I think like one." Kieran tapped his head. "You get to know them when you've fought with him as long as I have. Was in his squad when he was just a captain."

Aidan looked back to the command post. They were up on the hill in the early morning light on horses, activity going back and forth. Messengers came and went. Aidan couldn't keep anything straight.

At last, he turned back to the front and shrugged. "So you say."

"This'll be the last one, you'll see." Kieran pulled his coat closer. "We're too close to winter as is."

That was a prediction Aidan could get behind. He longed to go back home, get out of this infernal fighting.

Dawn rose red, the gold banner of the lion unfurling in the early morning breeze that bit just as deep with cold. Aidan rubbed his shoulders to keep warm, glad for the huddle of bodies around that helped.

Off in the distance, a white cloud was growing. He pointed it out to Lucas.

"They're here. Get ready, we're going up soon." He started checking his bow, looking for splits or cracks, not that there was any time left to do anything about it.

He turned out to be right, the sound of stamping feet rose over the hill beyond them, and the commanders started issuing their orders, getting the troops back into formation.

Aidan's squad was no exception, and they were ordered to unsling bows and prepare. He pulled a fresh bowstring from his oilcloth and bent the bow to string it.

He feared it would crack in the cold, like one man's did farther down the line, but keeping it close to his body had helped and he had no trouble.

Around him the others did the same, the creak of the bows and twang of the strings as they tightened, a kind of music of anticipation.

They weren't in the front lines like the infantry, but there were more than enough ways to get killed. Opposing arrows, cavalry, infantry. If the line broke, they'd be defenseless.

Well, almost defenseless. Aidan patted the long knife at his hip just to make sure it was there.

It was, and he finished in time to see the enemy army crest the hill, banners of the red eagle flying.

Aidan checked his quiver, counting the arrows. Never enough, but more than he'd had in the last battle. A skirmish, really. He twirled the shaft of one in his fingers until he was yelled at to put it away.

"Won't be long now," Kieran said. The wind had picked up from the west, and was going to affect the arrows.

Now the two battle lines were drawn, and silence reigned. Aidan shivered, not just from the cold, and it felt like a weight was hanging in the air.

No one said anything about how many were out there arrayed against them. No one had to.

They all had eyes, they could all see what he saw. With a sinking feeling in his heart, Aidan came to grips with the reality he wouldn't be going home tonight or ever again.

It was a shame. He wished he could bathe in the river again, so cold it made his skin tingle, or go hunting in the woods. Waiting beneath his favorite tree for the deer to walk by, sometimes for hours.

Then, the horns sounded. Someone from their side had been talking, but Aidan couldn't hear. Something about duty and fighting to the death, if he had to guess. It was usually like that before they fought.

The enemy advanced, and they were ordered ready. Aidan slid out an arrow, knocking it to the string. It would only be a few minutes now before they were in range.

And those minutes passed like a thick porridge in winter.

"Archers, ready," the sergeant shouted, repeating the command from farther down. Aidan raised his bow, looking at the distant trees for a gage of the wind's direction and strength. He adjusted a little to the east to compensate for it and picked his man, one in the front with a strange-looking helmet.

Busted, he guessed, but he couldn't tell from this far away.

"Aim." They were within range now, just barely. Most of the arrows would fall short, but some would make it. Aidan breathed in and out, controlling it like he had learned long ago.

"Loose!" He breathed out and let go, all the tension in his arm suddenly released with a twang.

The arrow brushed his cheek, a gentle touch, and then the wind of it ever so slight. The arrow sang out with the others, flying up into the air.

Aidan kept his eye on his mark, drawing his next arrow without thinking and pulling it back, straining against his arms. The cold was gone, long forgotten, and the arrows fell.

Before they hit, another volley was in the air. Aidan shifted his aim to the man next to him, seeing his shot strike true.

It was a grim victory, but a victory, nonetheless.

The enemy was running now, and Aidan was lost in aiming and firing, taking another bundle of arrows from a runner, and doing it all over again.

The two lines met with a clash, screams and metal ringing on metal. The red eagle tore through the front line, and now it wasn't volleys it was one by one shots.

Aidan kept his fire out from their line, although some weren't as skilled or careful, and the enemy arrows were falling into their infantry.

The sergeant was yelling at them to move up, but the infantry was being pushed back. There was nowhere to go but with them. Aidan grabbed another bundle of arrows, tripping on one but catching his balance, and went back until he had enough room to fire again.

Calvary were charging down the hill, led by a man in shining armor in front. They slammed into the infantry, parting them like a knife.

On a horse, the enemy made a more clear target. Aidan got to work, taking down one, then hitting another. That one kept on his horse until a spear-man took him down permanently.

Suddenly, the line parted in front, and the man in shining armor came roaring up to them. He was on the archers in seconds, cutting them down with a singing sword.

Only a small gap in his helmet was vulnerable. Aidan grasped his last arrow, pulled back, and aimed.

His arm was protesting, but he waited. The shining knight bared down on him, but Aidan focused on nothing but his breathing.

He loosed the arrow, then tried to scramble out of the way. The horse rode down on him faster than he could move, clipping him with a rock solid hit that ripped his bow from his hands and knocked his breath away.

The world spun, his arms flailing, and Aidan fell to the cold earth, blackness threatening to close in on his vision.

When he could breathe again, the cold smell of frozen earth was thick with hot blood. Men were yelling, a victorious cheer around him, and when he could move again he tried to take a look.

Pain lanced down his right arm and side, a pressure on his chest that made him gasp. The arm hung useless and made trying to get up almost impossible.

But then hands found him, helping him up, and he was back on his feet. Someone was yelling in his ear, pounding his back, and he yelled out in pain.

"Well done," another said. It was pure confusion, then Aidan looked around to see what had happened.

The cavalry were retreating, carrying a body on a horse surrounded by fighters. They had just made it back to their line and were swallowed up as he looked on. The banner was following them.

"Why are they leaving?" he asked as the group rode back up the hill. Trumpets called out from the opposing hill, ringing down a clear note.

"The prince is dead. Long live Unarcia!" Cheers rang out from the soldiers, mixed now with archers and infantry that were pushed back. The other army was in full retreat now, riding and running back through the battlefield.

Aidan looked for his company, struggling to see them through the mass of bodies. Sergeants and officers were yelling and beating, trying to restore order, and the front lines were following after the retreating forces.

Aidan asked around until he finally found his unit. He searched for Kieran, but no one had seen him since the cavalry had broken through the line.

Lucas was helping to tie up his useless arm, broken by the weight of the horse, when someone pointed to him.

A group of soldiers, angry looking and ready to fight, followed the finger toward him.

"What are the General's bodyguards doing here?"

"I don't know," Lucas whispered. A bolt of fear ran through him, remembering the extra ration of bread he had taken. He was hungry, and it didn't look like it belonged to anyone. He tried to keep his head down, but he had already been seen.

"On your feet," the hardest looking one said as they approached. Lucas shot to attention, and Aidan followed, slower and wincing. It hurt to stand upright.

The group parted, a young soldier pushed to the front. "Is this him?" another bodyguard asked.

"That's him. I saw it with my own eyes. It was his arrow."

Aidan's eyes widened, and hands clamped around him. "My arm," he cried. They readjusted their grip, then pulled him forward.

"What are you doing?" His sergeant asked.

"Leave him be. We have business with him. Keep your mouths shut about this," the angry one said.

"I didn't do anything, I swear," Aidan said as he was dragged through the army and back to the hill. They were taking him up to the command post, and men on horses waited, looking on.

"Hold your tongue," the angry one said. Aidan bit his lip, trying to lessen the pain of the jostling and the anticipation. What were they going to do to him? Would he be killed for stealing? It was only a little bread, and he had seen men do worse without punishment.

He was hungry.

They wouldn't answer his questions though, and soon he gave up. Resigning himself to his fate, he tried to keep up with the quick steps of his captors.

They were taking him to the General. There he sat, astride his horse, the famed sword Vanquish at his side, jewels shimmering in the afternoon.

The air was cool up here, and fresh. All the smells of the battlefield, the blood, the bile, the filth, were swept away by a gentle breeze from the north. Now, it smelled of pines and meadow deep in the grips of winter.

Aidan trembled as they stopped him before the General and his retinue. All faces were hard, worn by years of battle and the disappointments that it had brought.

"This is him?" The question came from one of the youngest of the group, still scarred across one cheek.

"Yes, my Lord."

He kept his mouth shut as his knees trembled. Aidan didn't know why he was here or what he had done.

Then, the General smiled. "Well done." He dismounted and reached out a hand.

Aidan stared at it until one of the General's guards elbowed him in the back. He took it, crushed by the grip, and shook hands with the General.

He felt dizzy, then surreal. It was like he was living through a strange mist, that everything was fuzzy.

"On behalf of the army of Unarcia, and the King who has bestowed his honor and duty upon me, I grant you the award of the Lion's Breath." The General reached to the shining gold necklace that glimmered, handed to him from one of his followers.

He put it around Aidan's neck, then let it rest upon his chest. Aidan licked his lips and swallowed to wet his dry throat. "What have I done to deserve this?"

A ripple of laughter ran through them, and the General smiled, breaking the corners of his eyes with creases. "You've killed the Prince, lad. And saved us from defeat at the same time."

"A well-placed arrow indeed," said the younger man. The next few minutes passed by like a dream, he was congratulated and whisked away to be treated, given clean cloths and a hot bath in the personal tents of the officers.

They left him the necklace, and he traced his good hand along it. The warmth of the bath soaked into him, dispelling the cold that he'd carried on the march for so long.

With a sigh, he dipped his body further underneath the water, and wondered in amazement at this turn of fortune.

# 4

## Forward Unto the Breach

Heavy into the breach we rushed ahead. My ears rang from the crash, the scent of gunpowder heavy in the air.

The first man took a bullet from my pistol, but the second was too fast. I slashed away his bayonet and cut into his throat, pushing him aside as he clutched at the red that flowed from it.

My blood-lust drowned out all thoughts but battle. The sounds of the fight faded, replaced by my own grunts and cries as I fought and bled.

Something tore into my shoulder, a sudden pressure, and I stuck my sword into the man's stomach. He didn't go down, so I had to hack away at his head until finally he slipped down to the dead.

I stumbled over the rubble and ruins of the wall. The cloud of dust and smoke still hung thick, lit up by flashes of light.

And then my companions were at my side, rushing forward into the cobbled streets that threatened to tip me onto the side.

Men were groaning or dead on the ground. I spat the iron tasting blood from my mouth, wiping my lips.

The street was mercifully clear.

"We go to the gate," I said. Pointing my sword, I urged the others on. I hoped that we were early enough to be in time.

"Where are they all?" Zurial asked. His neck dripped blood, but it wasn't his.

"Distracted, just like we planned." My foot caught an odd angle in the street, sending a momentary jolt up my leg, but after a stumble, I got up. Hands reached out, but I waved them away. "I'm fine."

We hurried, shouting and talking in the distance. I couldn't tell if it was ahead of us, beside, or behind.

We left the smoke, rushing into the clean smelling air again. Fire burned in the distance.

"They set fire to the city," Danthru said. I checked my gear and glanced around.

"There." We went up the stairs, ascending to the wall. More screams and clashes of weapons in the distance, flashes of powder and the report of rifles joined in.

We were exposed up here, and I didn't like it. But we were almost there, and the fighters at the wall saw us coming.

"Give 'em lead." I shot my own pistol, sending one careening off the wall to the street below. I tried to block out the sound of his impact, because they were on us in an instant.

They fought well, taking out at least four of us, but they were no match. I dispatched the last one with my sword and cleaned off the blood.

Now the way was clear to the tower that neighbored the gate. I waited with the others, hoping we hadn't drawn attention.

We hadn't.

The tower door was shut and locked, but a few swift kicks of Zurial's massive leg soon changed that.

We barged into a temporary hospital room, filled with wounded. Some of them tried to scramble to their feet to face us, but most were too far injured to do anything.

"I don't like this," Zurial said.

"Do it. We don't have time." I wanted to say *I'm sorry*, but I said nothing and thrust my sword into the closest rising soldier. I had to watch the light flicker and die in his eyes.

It made me sick to my stomach, no matter how many times I had seen it.

The others were dispatched quickly and quietly, then the way was clear. Our sharpshooters were doing their job on the opposing wall. Less than half of the soldiers were remaining than there should have been.

"Take aim, start with the ones on the end." Together we raised our pistols. There was a loud shot from the cannon. "Now."

Our volley rang true and men fell, struck by bullets. The soldiers next to them looked around, taken by surprise, but we were already reloading. Most continued to rain down fire on the army outside the gates, but one officer was searching for the cause of the attack.

"Don't turn back here," I pleaded, ramming home my bullet. But, it was of no use. He saw me, and shouting, turned his attention to us.

My bullet caught him in the throat, but the damage was done. The firing line turned on us, and there was no way to close the gap in time.

"Cover!" I threw myself down as bullets ripped over me. A few seconds later and I would have been riddled with them.

We tried to return fire, but had to retreat back to the safety of the tower. I scrambled in last, and just in time, as chips of rock sprinkled over me. The rest of our outfit was inside now, and I counted heads. Less than a dozen now. I would say a prayer for the dead later.

"We could use a miracle right now, couldn't we?" Danthru said. He grinned and pulled out a grenade, the only one we had brought with us.

I stopped him, a hand on his shoulder. "Wait, we don't want to use it just yet."

Pinned down, we took potshots at the soldiers.

"We can't stay here, they're calling for reinforcements," Zurial said. I cursed and shot another round, grateful to hear it hit true.

We had to do it. "Danthru, get over here." He brought the grenade, and we set it up, carefully removing the hole and inserting the wick.

Loathe to waste the costly armament, I gathered the remaining forces around to make a plan.

"We'll have to rush them, before they can recover, and hope that Danthru's aim is better than his boasting." That brought a few smiles, but not enough to make them heroes. "We'll line up in two rows."

After a little back and forth, the plan was ready. We were just getting into place when the tower shook violently and something exploded outside.

It rang my ears again, and when I could muster the strength to look outside, saw that half the wall was missing.

"That takes care of the soldiers," Zurial said.

"And complicates things." The walkway was destroyed, and the gate was just behind it, now out of reach. The four-foot gash in the wall made sure of that.

"We'll go anyway, before they can recover." Protests from behind me were cut short, and I sprinted out of the tower.

Things whizzed past my head, skittering and shattering occasionally, but I kept going. Everything I was carrying weighed on me, from my clothes to my sword and pistols, dragging me down, wanting to stop me.

But I kept going, lungs burning, heart pounding, I kept going. Only that door existed to me, the soldiers stumbling and staggering behind it. Blinded by the explosion, I would only have a few more seconds before they turned their attention my way.

So I ran and jumped the gap. For a pregnant moment that seemed to last forever I hung in the air, carried forward by momentum. The other side was so far, crumbling bricks reaching out to take me.

My body flew forward, and I made it to the other side, feet hitting the castle wall rocks and nearly flying back behind me.

I stumbled, legs pumping furiously, but then I caught my-self, bullets whizzing past my head.

Then, a few more steps to the door, and I was in. My shoulder caught the wood, smashing it into the surprised face of a soldier who tumbled back.

I loosed a volley at the nearest face, then sank my sword into another. The moment of surprise was over, the soldiers had paused but only a second, then were in action.

They fought back, defending the gate mechanism they knew I was after. I didn't stop, taking my wounds as well as giving them, fighting to get to it.

A soldier seized an axe, pulling it from a cubby, and ran to the rope. I couldn't let him get there, and struggled hand to hand with another, watching him go.

The fight demanded all my attention as my opponent's fist found my nose, smashing it and flooding my mouth with iron-tasting blood that overwhelmed my sense of smell. I punched him in the face, returning the favor with the hilt of my sword, feeling his nose and skull give way.

Battle cries behind me signaled the arrival of my allies, and it renewed the strength within me.

I cut deep into my opponents shoulder, drawing it down across his torso, which gave me a moment of respite.

I seized the advantage, drawing my remaining loaded pistol, sighting at the axe-wielding soldier's head, and feeling the world slow down.

He was all that existed in that moment, everything else around me slipping away. The axe was raised, ready to sever the rope and our last remaining chance at victory.

I breathed out, steadied my hand, ignoring the screams and yells around me, and squeezed the trigger.

The pistol flashed, the shot roared. Then, the man fell forward, axe clattering helplessly to the floor.

Zurial was beside me then, and Treles. "Open it," I said. Soldiers groaned around us, every last one incapacitated. I strode to the opposing door, pulling up the beam and sliding it into place.

We were locked in, at least on that side. And we had not a moment to lose. There were so few of us left, out of the dozens who had set out. Zurial, Treles, and Danthru were at the wheel, straining against it, and I sheathed my sword and joined them.

My shoulder pressed against the great arms, pushing them up and over. Again and again we strained, each time raising the mechanism to another click.

The weight of the gate was unbearable. There was pounding at the door, and shouts in a foreign language.

But outside there was a great cheer from our side, and it gave me strength, fueled the fire that burned within. "Push, push you dogs!"

I pushed. Step by step it raised. The door was being smashed now, glimpses of an axe breaking through, but the beam still held.

We had to do it. Click by click we worked.

Below me I saw into the gate, at the soldiers straining on the enemy side of it. They clutched at it, tried to keep it down, weighting it. The weight was overwhelming, but we kept going.

I was yelling now, every muscle in my body straining against the mechanism, every vein in my body pumping blood.

We couldn't let up now. "Danthru, the grenade." My eyes sought the door, half smashed, with arms reaching in to tear it apart.

His departure made the weight worse. The handle dug into my shoulder, forcing my body down.

It was painful, and I felt us losing ground. Danthru was lighting in now, sparks flying from his flint and tinder.

I almost smelled it as it caught, flaring up in a great burst that warmed my body. Danthru held it gingerly, took aim, then at the last possible moment, let fly.

I watched it sail through the air, praying that it would make it through the mass of bodies at the door.

By some miracle it disappeared, flying through the axe and hands that tore at the door. Lost from view I waited, anxiously, as the moment it should have detonated came and passed.

Danthru's face lost his smile, slipping.

Then light flashed, and flames leapt from the door. The sound deafened me, and I slipped to my knees.

The gate dropped, hovering a few inches lower, but Zurial caught it with both hands. He put two handles on his shoulders, one on each, and strained, yelling as he did.

I scrambled to my feet and joined him, as did the others. Danthru threw his weight into the mechanism and it shifted, raising back again.

Zurial's massive legs strained, veins popping and sweat pouring out of them. He pushed, we pushed, and the mechanism moved.

Inch by inch we raised the gate, until at last the defenders below could hold on no longer, harassed and attacked by our side. When they let go the mechanism shot forward, and we quickly rammed the thing home and locked it.

Below us our army poured through, cutting through the defenders and pouring lead and sword into them.

They flooded the streets, an angry beehive that had finally been loosed. Like a wave they swept through the defenders and made them flee, turning up the embattlements and clearing away any who tried to defend.

My strength was spent, as was the others, but we pulled ourselves to the windows and watched them. The other door was ruined with death and destruction, and nothing was left alive.

"We did it boys. We did it." I slumped onto a barrel, taking a moment to recover. Smoke rose from below, that taste of gunpowder sharp on it.

"They'll be talking about us tonight," Danthru said.

"And I'll pay for the extra rations myself, if I have to." So many lost, but we had done it. "The fight's over. Now, we get to go home."

# 5

## GENERAL

He surveyed the battlefield, the crisp northern wind ruffling his hair and burning through his cloak with the cold, but he ignored it.

"Have the  cavalry stage up on the right flank, and the archers halfway up the hill. We want them drawn in as close as we can before they start firing."

"Do you expect them to set up camp?"

"No, they'll come on a forced march overnight. Which gives us some hope, if not much." Two hills, with a killing field in between. What would tomorrow hold?

"I'll be in my tent for the night. Gentlemen, this is our last stand. If the eagle advances any farther there will be no hope. You know what to do, I expect you to do your duty." The fresh scent of the pines blew in, dispelling the filthiness of the camp and army behind. He wouldn't sleep well tonight.

◆○◆

They roused him early, far before the morning light, as ordered. The chill of the morning was a bite, even in the tent warmed by a small fire, a luxury even for him. His joints creaked and ached from the cold as he sat up, then stood.

It had been a restless night, like so many before, but the taste of battle was on his lips now, and the anticipation that came with it. There would be glory today, only he hoped it would be on his side.

The rest of the army was still sleeping, except for the picket and sentries that surrounded the camp and kept everything safe. He dressed, his squires helping him to buckle on the armor, foregoing the helmet. The steel was cold, and it sucked the heat right out of his skin wherever it touched him. He adjusted his undergarment to cover his neck where it still was.

Then, out into the cold morning he went. The wind almost tore the tent flap out of his hand with a gust, then went silent.

"General, a messenger from the scouts came this morning," said David, his aid.

"Bring him forward." A young scout, scrawny and ill-equipped for the cold, walked forward shivering. The light from a torch cast half his face in shadow, tight.

"S-Sir," the messenger stuttered. "We saw the enemy approaching." He produced a letter and held it out.

"How far out?" The General nodded and his aide took the letter, handing it to him. He examined the exterior, turning it over in the light.

"Less than a day's march."

The General narrowed his eyebrows. "Give this man something warm to drink. Please, relax." A cup was produced and filled with steaming tea.

"How many?"

"The entire army." The messenger was still nervous but having something to hold seemed to soothe him. Somewhere off in the distance a bird called in the night, lone and solitary. A puff of wind stirred the tent, then died down. "Four regiments of infantry, same of archers. Three or more of cavalry."

"They'll be here in the morning, won't they?"

"Y-yes sir." His hands trembled, shaking his cup.

"No fault of your own." He raised a hand, and a servant came over. "See to this man, give him a hot meal and a good rest. We'll need everyone we can get." The General patted him on the shoulder. The man was whisked away, and the General continued on his track to the main tent.

He was the first one there, but not for long. Before he could finish filling his pipe and lighting it Marnger stepped in through the flap, shivering and stamping his feet.

"Good morning, sir."

"Thomas, morning." The General took a wick from the lantern, letting it flare up with a yellow tail of fire, then set it to his pipe and puffed. The smoke was hot and tickled his tongue, the sweet and tangy taste of it filling his mouth.

He puffed out, extinguishing the wick and snapping shut the lantern cover. "I heard the news. Nowhere to turn this time, is there?" the General asked.

"I'm afraid not." A few more trickled in, and bade him greeting, gathering around the map table. "He's got us, but we have him at the disadvantage. I aim to use the hills to our advantage, make him earn his attack."

Simon, the youngest captain, frowned. A battle scar raked across his cheek, a badge of honor earned against this very enemy. "What hope is there with half their numbers?"

"There is always hope, Simon. No matter the odds, we have the chance to fight. Unless we give up, we'll always have that chance." The General drew a deep mouth of smoke, blowing it out. "I know this is a dark morning. We might not have their numbers, but we have the skill."

He tapped the bottom of his pipe on the table, sprinkling a tiny bit of ash on the map. The edges were worn, parts frayed. The trail ended here, at the entrance of Unarcia's Southern pass. If they fell, the rest of Unarcia would follow. "The enemy is far from home, with overstretched supply lines. Their troops are losing the will to fight, deserting in larger numbers every day. Thank you."

Taking the offered letter, he unfolded it in their presence.

"They'll never make it past us," Marnger said, his armor creaking as he moved his hands.

"Easier said than done. Your boldness requires action to accompany it," Trevor said.

"Enough. We've more than enough fighting to go around," The General said. He looked each man in the eye. Despite the tension, they worked well together, which was one of the reasons they were still fighting. "Now, this is the final council before the battle. Let's go over it again."

They stepped out of the tent in the early morning, dawn still hours away. The alert had sounded while they were still inside, and men were forming up into ranks on the hastily constructed parade ground now.

There would be no warm breakfast for them. The chill of the morning swept through him, but he ignored it. They wouldn't be the only ones.

He looked up, off in the distance toward the capitol. There were lives there that depended on him, and all the others, standing their ground.

Ashes fell from his upturned pipe, a few still glowing. He stamped them out, grateful for the movement in his limbs to help keep him warm. His armor sucked the heat out of him, despite the leather under trappings, not to mention the aching in his joints.

Nevertheless, he strode out to the horse line, mounting on Tizone after a quick pet and a few whispers of encouragement.

She was showing her age now, graying around her black mane, but she still was the most dependable horse he had ever known. The leather creaked as he mounted, and he wondered if he would ride her to the last.

For that may be today.

With the rest of the command, he watched the army form up under the cool night sky. There wasn't a cloud above them, and he was grateful for the view.

He longed to be back on his estates, nestled in the big bed he shared with his wife. Sighing, he almost felt the soft doublet and sheets of lamb's wool against his skin, and how well they warmed him.

A few minutes later the lines were formed, and the column was advancing. It took less than a half hour to get them to the hill, the infantry and archers in the front with the cavalry behind.

They needed more time to get the horses fed and ready, but the foot soldiers needed only to gather their equipment and march. They went with the column, not bothering to wait for the horse, and arrived an hour or so before dawn.

The command group peeled off just before the hill, taking their vantage point on the tallest point just before the forest. They waited, exchanging the pleasantries of anticipation and a hard day ahead.

Loved ones were discussed, as well as what each would do when the war was over. The General didn't take part, preferring to allow them their hopes and dreams.

He had to focus on the task at hand.

The sky was beginning to lighten when the cavalry arrived, peeling off their two columns to take the right flank upslope. The General surveyed the chosen battlefield, the best location he could think of this close to the capitol.

They were surrounded on both sides by the Green Mountains and had taken vantage on a gently sloping hill that went into the valley. A small stream trickled along the bottom, before it went up at a faster grade to another hill.

That was where they would be coming from and would be forced to meet them under fire as they advanced.

It might not be enough.

He sat on his horse, letting the cold seep into his body and dive down deep into his bones. It would be soon. It would be here.

The General pulled up his cloak tighter against his skin, letting the others talk in their nervous state. They needed to know there were others around, that they weren't the only ones feeling the anticipation and dread that he was feeling.

They had been fighting so long he didn't even remember what peace was like. What a summer without campaigns and blood, without battles and death could even be.

There was always the hope of peace after each fight, and the dread of failure before each one as well.

He felt it now, the tickle at the back of his mind. They hadn't prepared enough. They weren't ready. They were too few, their opponent too many.

He was a failure, and his failure would mean the death of men. For that he mourned in the cold morning as the sun lit up the black sky to gray. He bowed his head, searching for a God to pray to and found nothing.

What good would it be, now at the end of his life? A flash of knowledge flew into him. This would be his final day in this land, his last alive. Tomorrow would find him cold and in the grave. As cold as the frost on the trees and the ice in the ground.

They would dig him a whole, and the earth would swallow him up dead. He grimaced at the thought, ground his teeth to distract himself.

The sun crested the horizon, casting a brilliant array of colors into the clouds. It took away the fears for a second, eased his pain.

So he watched, sitting on his horse, and waited.

A messenger pounded up. "The army's coming." The General waved him away with a fatherly nod. He had seen their approach off in the distance and thought he might hear the echo of the footsteps of thousands of men and horse.

"Ready the lines," he ordered, and his order was relayed to each of his subordinates in turn. Riders were dispatched from the top of the hill, rushing to each cluster of troops and bands of fighting men.

They swarmed like ants below, gathering up their arms and forming into a great line that stretched at the top of the hill. The accompanying sound of chaos and order floated up to them, and he relished it.

This would be the last battle morning. The last rush of excitement and battle lust. This would be the end of the army, or complete victory.

In a short time everyone was ready, the non-combatants pulled back far behind, and all they could do was wait.

He patted Tizone, rubbing her neck and soothing her. She stamped her feet, letting the blood flow back to them to drive out the cold. He let her, just as the enemy came into view.

It took his breath away. There were more than he expected, even more than they'd reported. His stomach dropped.

He spotted the leaders at the front as they reached the edge of the forest. They held back and pulled off to one side, letting the infantry and archers move into position ahead of them. The cavalry they left in the forest line, hiding their real numbers for view.

They streamed out, and it felt like hours before they took their lines and made them solid. Banners of the red eagle streamed, mocking him.

They didn't belong here. They deserved to be driven out as invaders and enemies. But, so far, he had failed to do that.

And it had come to this.

He roused himself, giving the last few orders to his men. "And Ethan?"

"Yes General?"

"Hold off the cavalry until my order. No matter what you do, keep them in reserve." Something flickered across Ethan's face. That argument had gone poorly, but he at least got his point across.

"Understood, General." He saluted and kicked his horse into a gallop, sending puffs of frost up with every footfall.

"And now, we wait." The enemy was still getting into final position, orders shouting and horns sounding.

Tension was thick in the air even more than usual. The enemy knew their numbers, would press their advantage as much as possible. One would have to be a fool not to see it.

The last flurry of orders was finished, and silence fell on the group. The horses sensed it, whinnying once and trembling, then falling silent as well.

What went through his mind at that time surprised him. Memories of his family, his training, and his first command. How fearful he had been standing in that line, holding that sword, when the enemy pressed forward.

The fear was different now, blunted by the years. There was still a chance of death, no doubt, but there were two dozen lines of men in between them. No, now the stakes were an entire nation and the peoples that occupied it, and a raging and vengeful King that already had little confidence in his ability.

Then, the horns sounded and brought him out of his memories and fears.

"So it goes," he said. The words were caught on the wind and carried away into the fresh, morning sky.

What a day to witness such bloodshed. The scent of the pines and horses intermingled with a mass of unwashed troops below. All would be swept into blood and filth in minutes.

The first line of the enemy advanced, walking downhill. They were still out of range, but the archers prepared, nocking arrows to their bows and raising them.

The enemy general and his retinue stayed close to the tree line, and he watched them carefully. Maddox was a capable general and a worth adversary. He knew that the slope would give them trouble, and he knew that he knew it. He would have something in surprise for him, and the General guessed it would be a cavalry charge.

They would be able to make up the ground quickly, but it would mean pulling his infantry apart if he attacked from the middle or shifting them if he attacked from the flank.

And the right flank was protected by his own cavalry, ready and standing in the opening for all to see. The left flank would be harder to attack, the slope steeper and far more difficult to advance on while under fire.

Arrow flew now, falling on the infantry as they entered the valley. They broke into a run but had to go uphill. The distance was far enough to get in at least three or four volleys, enough to soften them up.

The whistles of the arrows continued, falling into the ranks of infantry. Movement at the tree line caught his attention.

"General, they advance their cavalry," Simon said. Armor glinted in the sunlight, flashing steel that weighed down the armored cavalry. A portion of the command team peeled off.

"The Prince is here." The General furrowed his brow. This was a surprise, and unanticipated. The prince had always been bold and brash, but the wisdom of King Littlearm held him from battle most of the time.

Unless they knew they had all the advantage and thought it would be an easy fight.

His standard merged with the cavalry, and he took up his place at the front. "Keep an eye on him," the General said. Screams and clashing swords brought his attention back to the front lines.

The arrows had helped, but the infantry was still too many. "Sir, the cavalry?" Bartholomew was at his arm then, whispering. There was fear in his voice.

"No, not yet." The enemy calvary was at the crest of the hill. This was the critical moment, when they would commit. They headed for the center, and signal horns blew.

The infantry split, as he thought they would, a majority peeling away to expose the center. The enemy charged downhill, covering ground far faster than they needed to. The prince was in the lead, sword flashing and raised.

"He fights with courage." As he said it, he knew that they would not be able to defend against him.

The cavalry charged up the slope and slammed into the unprepared infantry like a hammer. Men screamed, bodies flew, and they continued on as if there was nothing in their way, the prince at the front.

"Send in our cavalry," the General said. A rider ran off with the order, and seconds after he reached the line, their own cavalry rushed out to meet them.

That was the last of his reserve, and not enough to save them. The prince was inspiring his army, leading them in attack and onto victory.

With a tight chest, he looked on. the smells of the battlefield reached them now. Blood. Too much blood, and bile and filth mixed together. Men would empty themselves when they died, making the most horrible smell.

He hated it with a passion.

Anger rose inside him, fueled by hatred. He wouldn't see his family again. He would be done after this, the whole kingdom would.

In a moment his sword was out. With a quick flick of his ankles he spurred Tizone to a gallop.

His retinue protested, calling after him, but he didn't care. This was no moment for concern, no time for caution. There was only one way they could have a chance to win now.

If he managed to kill the prince.

"For Unarcia!" He galloped past the waiting line of support and medics, and a cheer followed him. He hoped his example would keep the fraying army from falling apart. The sides of the line were already bulging, falling in.

They wouldn't hold for long.

His banner-man caught up to him, then blew his horn as they rushed for the breach together.

Now it was wind in his hair, stinging cold biting at his face. The warm sun on his flesh pulled him forward, the warm anger in his heart keeping him going.

"Unarcia!" The cheers rose up, louder, infecting the army from the back to the front. The infantry held, trying to close up the gash the cavalry had made, and his own cavalry hammered the enemies left flank.

Even though he had crossed half the distance to his lines, it wouldn't be enough. The enemy cavalry were already to the archers, despite the arrows they were shooting.

It would only be a few more minutes until they were completely through, splitting the army in two and weakening it.

He wasn't sure they would be able to last long after that, not with the numbers they were up against.

There was nothing he could do but watch, the feeling of failure bubbling up inside, and the resignation of defeat floating on top of it.

He closed his eyes, feeling the gallop of Tizone beneath him, the wind rushing past. His ears were filled with the sounds of battle. Men screaming, horses crying, metal on metal.

Then, something strange happened. There was an odd cry of victory going up in front of him.

He couldn't believe it at first, but opened his eyes anyway. The cavalry was retreating, pulling back. Something had happened.

He pulled up his horse, let the others catch up to him in a trot. "What happened?"

"The Prince, sir, he went down. I couldn't see anything other than that," Ethan said. *Curious.*

Helped by his own forces, the cavalry turned and carried the prince and his horse between them down the hill. Now his own cavalry was harassing them, and the infantry on the enemy's left flank, forcing them back.

The infantry was following, peeling back from the attack. Horns were blowing in the distance across the valley. The General pulled his horse up short, less than a stone's throw from the front lines. The archers at the back were talking and yelling, great whoops of victory going up against the darkened sky.

Vultures flew overhead. *You'll get your feast,* he thought, surveying the bodies that were stacked up high. In the short amount of fighting both sides had lost too many.

But he noted with grim satisfaction, they had given far more than they had got. "Pull back the troops, don't let them harry them too long," he said, dispatching a messenger.

"And bring me whoever brought down the prince. We've got more than an award to give him. We might owe him our very lives." The sun broke through the clouds that had gathered, lightening the mood and his own heart.

It was too late in the season for them to try and push forward. Not without a leader like this. He looked to the enemy command, who was turning back into the woods. There would be a fight for power, of that he was sure.

He hoped that General Maddox wouldn't win. Of all the men he would least like to meet on the field of battle, he was the highest on his list.

Catching his breath after a short ride he leaned back to ease his aching back. It had been a rough year, and he looked forward to a warm bath. Thinking about those steaming tubs made him ache all the more, but a smile broke on his face, nonetheless.

He had managed to survive once again.

# Eclectic Stories

Thank you for spending your precious time reading this book.

If stories make you salivate, learn more about lore, take an exclusive sneak peek behind the scenes, and get writing updates in my newsletter, Eric's Eclectic Stories.

As a bonus you'll get *Stories from the Deep*, a Patmos Sea Fantasy Adventure anthology that gives a glimpses of lore, extra prologues and epilogues, and character backstories.

If you aren't satisfied, unsubscribe at any time.

Join at erickercher.com.

-Eric Kercher

# Also By Eric Kercher

## Patmos Sea Fantasy Adventure Series

*Fathomless Pursuit*
*Architect's Prize*
*Ironbound Path*
*Sunken Prey*
*Unanswered Prophecy*
*Hardened Pilgrim*
*Final Peace*

## Seventh Hall Chronicles

*Seventh Hall*
*Ode to the Survivors*
*Bastion of the Deep*

## Epic of Hornblood Castle

*Siege of the Unfinished Keep*
*Winter at Hornblood*
*Branch of the Everlong*

## Anthologies

*Red Eagle Anthology*

# About Author

Eric Kercher was born and raised in a small town on the Great Plains on good books. After attending a small state school on the east coast he joined the US Navy to serve his country and explore the world. He worked on submarines, and the world beneath the waves captivated him with all its mysteries and wonders. After spending time in larger cities, he's settled down in a quiet town with his wife and children. When not on an adventure in a good book the author enjoys creating dust woodworking, architecture, and spending time with loved ones.

Find out more at www.erickercher.com.